The Pit

The Hisime Ara Chronicles

Book Two

The Pit

The Hisime Ara Chronicles
Book Two

By Misty D. Billman

short
STUFF
publishing

Short Stuff Publishing

Copyright © 2016 By Misty D. Billman

Cover Art by Jimmy Nijs

Book Design by Misty D. Billman

Page Art and Cover Design by Melissa Johnson

Printed in the United States of America

First Printing, 2016

ISBN 978-0-9899364-3-9

ISBN 978-0-9899364-5-3

Short Stuff Publishing L.L.C.

Aurora, CO 80011

To Marvin

For pushing me.

are

Other Books By Misty D. Billman

The Prophecy of Kalodorim

REVELATIONS (Book One)
DISCIPLES (Book Two) *Coming soon.*
UNTITLED (Book Three) *Coming soon*

The Hisime Ara Chronicles

Royal Elves (Book One)
The Pit (Book Two)
Old Mine (Book Three)

Other Books By Short Stuff Publishing

THE DEAD OAK

By Marvin Visher

CONTENTS

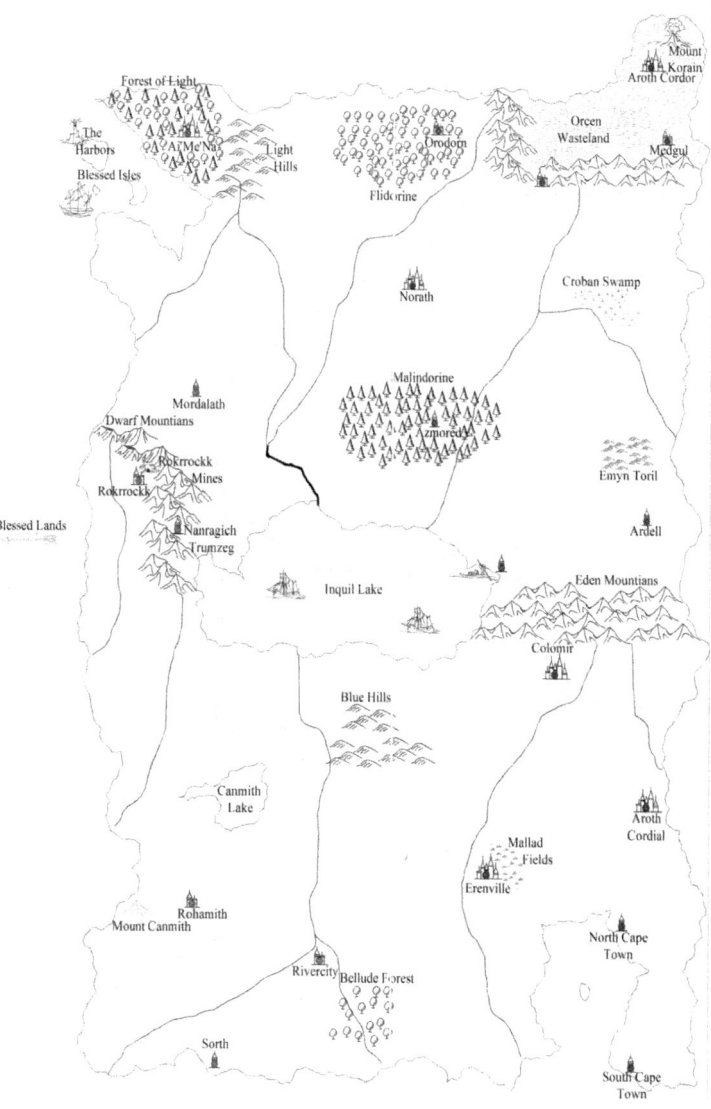

Mount
Korain
Aroth Cordor

Forest of Light

The
Harbors

Blessed Isles

Al'Me'Nar

Light
Hills

Orcen
Wasteland

Medgul

Orodorn

Flidorine

Croban Swamp

Norath

Malindorine

Mordalath

Azmored

Dwarf Mountians

Emyn Toril

Rokrrockk
Mines

Rokrrockk

Ardell

Nanragich
Trumzeg

Blessed Lands

Inquil Lake

Eden Mountains

Colomir

Blue Hills

Canmith
Lake

Aroth
Cordial

Mallad
Fields

Erenville

Rohamith

Mount Canmith

North Cape
Town

Rivercity

Bellude Forest

Sorth

South Cape
Town

PART ONE

HISIME STOOD OUTSIDE THE ROOM WITH HER eyes closed. Leaning against the wall next to the door she listened intently to the conversation on the other side. They always forgot about her superhuman hearing which came from choosing to be an Elf some twenty years ago now. The changes, called the *Kanolay*, were slow but they were there and because of the Elf hearing, she could hear every single word.

"She isn't ready, Calabmore," Commander Pannor said.

"You are wrong, Pan," Calabmore said. "She is

beyond ready. She's been training longer than anyone else. She and I started at the same time and I am a captain and you haven't even sent her on a mission yet."

"You were already partly trained when you got here. She lacks confidence," Commander Pannor pointed out.

Pannor was right though, she wasn't ready. It was great that Calabmore—her only brother—believed she was ready, but facts were facts, and she wasn't ready. Calabmore always thought her more capable than she was. When they were still under their evil guardians' care, he tried to help her escape and she ended up back at their house, granted it was for the best, but she couldn't even run away the right way, even from the beatings and malnourishment that she suffered every day.

She'd learned the Rangers art slowly and her confidence had come even slower. It was true that she was half-Elf, and had chosen to be an Elf, but she had spent a good portion of her life being put down and trampled upon. It wasn't that easy to gain self-confidence and it didn't help that she was a slow learner. It had taken her twice as long as her brother to learn how to track animals.

Calabmore was the whole reason she had joined the Rangers. He didn't want to be an Elf like she did. He wanted to be like their father Celebmir and was proving to be the perfect Ranger, just as their father was. She, however, was not.

"Because, other than me and Lord Melrim, no one has ever given her any confidence. Twenty years, Pan, twenty years and you still have her sparing the novices in the sword yard."

In Pannor's defense, she thought, her parry's

were still a little weak and she couldn't quite get down the Elf on the Mountain stance.

"Fine, Calabmore, but if she fails this, she's out. I never should have taken her in the first place. The battlefield is no place for a lady."

"The Elves have female warriors."

"We are not the Elves."

"But she is."

Pannor gave a loud sigh, she could almost hear the hairs on his van dyke blow in his breath. "She can take the case of Jepith Hillfast."

"The petty thief?" Calabmore ask.

"Yes, he has run and no one knows where too. A Ranger should be able to track him easily enough."

"Very well. I will let her know, Pan."

She could hear his boots making way toward the door. She moved quietly from the wall and started heading down the hall. With any luck her brother would think it was just coincidence that she was walking down that hall at that particular time.

"Hisime!" he called. She looked back and smiled acting surprised.

"Hello, Calabmore."

"Pannor has a mission for you. Isn't that great!" he exclaimed. His whole face lit up. He wanted this so badly for her, she didn't have the heart to tell him what she really thought.

"Really?" she said in mock surprise, hoping it was enough to fool him. "What is it?"

"A guy named Jepith Hillfast. He's a petty criminal, mostly steals from venders off the street. He ran from the guards of Ardell a few days ago. Since we are here, the guards asked Pannor to get a Ranger to track him down. Pannor thought of you."

Hisime wanted to laugh, but that would blow her cover and give away the fact that she overheard the two talking. She nodded instead. Her biggest fear was letting her brother down and this might just do it.

She brushed a strand of her long brown hair back behind her slightly pointed ear. "Sounds good. When do I leave and what information do I get?"

"You will leave in the morning. Pannor is waiting for you in his office to give you more information on who you are looking for and all that good stuff."

"Thank you, sir." She saluted him with her left fist to her chest. It was so hard to be professional around her brother. She wanted to put him in a headlock and ruffle his hair. His van dyke was still growing back after she shaved it off in his sleep a few days back.

Instead, she just stood there like a good solider speaking to her commander. He nodded slightly and turned to leave.

As he walked away, she couldn't believe how lucky she had gotten; he didn't know she had been eavesdropping. A smirk spread across her face as she started back toward Commander Pannor's office.

"Oh and, Hisime," her brother called. She turned to see his green eyes shimmering. "Next time you eavesdrop move away from the door a bit faster and a bit more quietly."

Boran Forain, that man knew everything.

With a smile he turned again. She shook her head and continued her march toward her commander's office. Knocking gently, she took a deep breath and closed her eyes.

"Come in." She opened her eyes and stepped inside.

The meeting with Commander Pannor Talon was quick and to the point. Hisime could tell he didn't want her going on this minor mission, and she honestly didn't really want to go, but her brother wanted it so badly and had argued so hard for her, she couldn't say no. Commander Pannor spoke to her as if he had eaten something sour and then dismissed her without so much as a smile.

The parchment he had given her with the case information wasn't more than a couple of pieces and she had already scanned it a few times over, before packing her things.

Now she stood in her tavern room looking to see if she had missed anything. Her saddlebags sat on the small bed in the middle of the room. There wasn't much in them, or in the room itself.

She stood with one hand on her hip and the other scratching her head when a knock came to her door. She quickly called for the person to come in.

"All ready I see," Calabmore said looking around, his green eyes glowing. "This has been a long time coming. I am so glad to see it."

"There are fifty others he could have chosen who would do a better job than I."

"Nonsense, Hisime. You will do great." He hugged her. "You have been in training for a very long time. You just need the confidence to do this, to be better—to be the best. I know you can do it."

Suddenly she flashed back to the old log cabin they had grown up in. Her brother was giving her another pep talk just to get her through the day. Her guardians had beaten her and worked her to the bone everyday she was in that house while her brother was treated like a king. Calabmore had been her only shining star and was always there to talk her down, or up—or whatever direction she needed.

"Hisime?"

"Sorry, memories." she said softly.

"Narnim and Sayrah?" he asked softly. She

shook her head to say no.

Narnim and Sayrah. She hadn't seen them since their trial, which didn't last long; they were given ten years in an Elven jail. It wasn't exactly a harsh punishment, but it wasn't too lenient either. Hisime was satisfied with the sentence and moved on with her life as best she could. The flashbacks happened often though.

"Then what?" he asked.

"You. Just thinking about how you have always been my hero,"

"Nah, Melrim is your true hero."

"I haven't seen him in two years." She frowned.

Melrim was her boyfriend and it was true they hadn't seen each other in two years, but that was normal. Their jobs often had them both traveling and nowhere near each other. They kept in contact through letters delivered by carrier hawks. Melrim truly was one of her heroes—he had been the one who freed her from her evil guardians and brought her to the Elves. The fact that he fell in love with her surprised her even more, as, until then, no one but her brother had ever loved her.

"Still your boyfriend," he retorted. "And what is two years to Elves?"

"Two years is two years."

"To me two years can be quite a long time, but I will never see the eternities. You, however, will, and two years is but the blink of an eye."

"I am forty years old, not four thousand like Orodorn."

"I know, but I am just saying." He sighed and ran his fingers through his hair. "Well, this got depressing. I love you Hisime and you will do great."

"I hope so."

PART TWO

HISIME ARA JUMPED OFF HER HORSE AND RAN her fingers through her long brown hair with a hefty sigh. She was utterly lost. There was no way she could have ended up on the east coast, but there it was, she gazed upon it with her blue eyes. A vast ocean of blue-green water and white foam lapping against the shore. She watched as birds fished in the ocean. Some of the fish jumped out of the water to get a tasty bug for themselves. Behind her laid nothing. The vast open plains of dead grass lay behind and she could see for miles. How did she get herself so lost?

She would have to back track all the way to the hills and restart from there. How could someone training with the Rangers for the last twenty years get so lost? She could track, she could sword fight, she could tell direction by the sun, the stars, and other noticeable signs. How did she get so lost? She growled at herself and hopped back onto her horse. She stroked the horse's mane softly.

Hisime just could not figure out where she had gone wrong. Following tracks was normally easy for her. It was one of the very first things she picked up on when she first came to train with the Rangers. Looking back over the past few days, she remembered taking the right path to begin with. She went over the information Pannor had given her so many times she had memorized it. He went off toward Emyn Toril and from there a path should emerge as there was no road going to or from since it was not a normal path of commerce. Once close to the hills, she had found a path that was clearly not made by animals and began to follow it, it led her to the sea.

"Sorry, girl, looks like we have to start over. Boy, my brother is never gonna let me live this one down, is he?" She smiled at the thought of her brother. Then she took the reins and turned her horse around.

She left the shore and headed inland. Three days out from Ardell, and still not a single clue as to the criminal's whereabouts. She should have found some sign of him by now. But that was assuming she had gone in the right direction, and all evidence was pointing to the contrary. She'd have to double back and head toward the hills instead, and find some way to quickly make up the distance.

She stopped her horse Bunny after an hour or so and tied her up to a tree. She placed the feed bag on the horse's head and patted her down. After a quick rub down, Hisime went to find fire wood for a fire to heat her food. She'd shot a rabbit earlier in the day and that would be her dinner. She was tired of the jerky and cheese she brought with her. After all, this wasn't supposed to be taking her so long anyway.

After she got the fire going with her flint and steel, she made quick work of skinning and gutting the rabbit. It wasn't her favorite food, venison was much tastier, but she wouldn't have been able to carry a deer around for a few hours, besides she hadn't even seen one.

Her Elven family didn't exactly approve of her carnivorous appetite, but she had been raised by Men and was now training with them. Besides, she didn't have time to go hunting for berries. Well, ok maybe she did. Right now she had rabbit though.

She pulled out some spices from her saddlebags and slowly seasoned the rabbit as it cooked over the small fire.

"Keep the fire small, it's not cold you don't need much heat Hisime," she reminded herself. "The smaller the fire the less obvious you are. Right, Bunny?" The horse ignored her and she shook her head with a small smirk. No, it was always a good idea to keep a small fire. Orcs could be roaming anywhere. Or, worse yet, fletchers or *Nevodluga*. She had never seen any of those creatures in person but she had heard plenty about them. She did not want to get caught alone with any of them. That much she knew.

After the short dinner break she cleaned up and continued on. It was lonely riding alone. She'd never been alone for so long in her life. She kept trying to convince herself that she truly was alone but she heard leaves rustling and sticks snapping and found her mind racing. It was very possible that it was all in her brain—Calabmore had warned her about hearing things when she was out here alone. She hadn't believed him then but she was starting to now. Plus, her advanced Elf ears picked up more than normal Human ears and it was still something she was getting used to.

She hadn't always had the Elves sense of hearing. It was something that was developing along with her keener eyesight. She had chosen to be an Elf a mere twenty years ago—ok, it had seemed like forever ago now, but she had to start thinking in the eternal sense—and since choosing to be an Elf her body was starting to transform. It wasn't a lot at once. In fact, it was slow and steady. She grew into her new slimmer body, she grew into her better eye sight, and she grew into her better hearing. Height, however, was not changing, much to her dismay. Nevertheless, the augmented senses still gripped her as remarkable and new more often than not. She also didn't trust them quite yet either. Often, her thoughts took her to how she would look when all the changes were finished.

As the sun began to set, she realized she had missed her chance to set up camp in the light. She cursed at herself for getting lost in her thoughts again—that's probably how she got lost in the first place. Her mind wanders too much. *Forain*.

She swiftly found a place to make camp and tied up Bunny before starting another small fire. It may have been spring time but nights on the plains could get cold and it helped to keep predators away. *Nevodluga*. She rolled out her bed roll and grabbed her journal.

Her brother had insisted on her keeping a journal, so she'd written in it every night for the past twenty years. It did help her become more proficient in reading and writing, which she guessed was good. She had gone twenty years without needing to read or write but she had to admit it was coming in handy now.

Today I royally messed up by getting lost. I am not even sure how that happened. I was following the tracks as I always have—as I was taught to. I have never messed up like this before. I have always been one of the top trackers in my training groups. I feel like I am letting Calabmore down. He has done so much for me, and here I am letting him down, again. I will never be able to repay my ~~little~~ younger brother.

I am a failure just like Narnim and Sayrah always said I was. I always thought I would be able to get over the abuse they put me through, and yet here I am still feeling like I need to make them proud. And again I have failed Calabmore and Melrim alike by caring about what the vile scum thinks. Why do I always disappoint them? I am worthless. I want to stop feeling this way, I want to amount to something, to prove my guardians wrong, but I fear I never will and they will forever be right.

Melrin always tells me I need to think more of myself. He says he wishes I could see myself the way he sees me—but I can't. Even twenty some years later, all I can think of is what was pounded into my head as a child and teenager. You are a failure, Hisime Ara. You are no good, Hisime Ara. You are rubbish, Hisime Ara.

Why was it so much harder to accept what Melrin and Calabmore said over what the vile moose excrement pounded into my brain?

Another failure.

With a sigh, she closed the journal and placed it back in her saddlebags.

She took care of Bunny as hastily as she could, while still making sure not to overlook any little detail. A well-cared for horse took care of you as much as you took care of them. That had been pounded into her head by Melrim.

She sighed again. She missed Melrim. She pulled out the last letter she'd received from him and curled up in her bed roll before she quickly drifted off to sleep.

SHE AWOKE TO A NOISE. SHE DIDN'T KNOW HOW long she had slept or what the sound she'd heard was either. She sounded like a small snap. Maybe a branch breaking or a twig? No, it wasn't quite crisp enough to be a broken branch. She looked around and didn't see much. It was completely dark out, even with the moon high in the night sky.

She got up and looked around for something—anything. But other than her and her horse, she saw nothing. She tried to look for tracks but there were none. She bit her lip as she kept looking. Was she imagining things again? Maybe it had been a dream?

She looked to Bunny who was still sleeping and frowned. Walking slowly back over to her bed roll, she laid down again. But this time, she stayed awake listening for anything out of the ordinary. She heard only the normal night sounds—crickets and leaves in the breeze. The sound of the fire crackling as it died.

She knew she wouldn't sleep, so she got up and threw more wood into the fire, watching as the flames consumed the wood slowly. It turned black as it burned and crackled. It was oddly hypnotizing.

She finally resigned herself to drift back into a dreamless sleep. Her awareness still heightened though.

WHEN SHE WOKE AGAIN IT WAS MORNING, JUST after dawn. Birds were chirping instead of crickets and Bunny was standing around already looking ready for the day.

Hisime rose and started to pack things up. She took care of Bunny and got ready for the day. She poured some of her water on the fire to make sure it was out, then covered the embers with dirt. She was having a cold meal for breakfast on the saddle. She needed to get back on track. She had to find Jepith.

Climbing up onto Bunny, she started north again. She pulled out some dried meat and cheese and gnawed on them as she rode. She wasn't sure she was ever going to find this guy. All she had was the location he had last been seen.

She gave an exasperated sigh. Why did her brother think she could do this?

As she rode, she kept an eye on her surroundings and listened for any sound that might be out of the ordinary. She was sure it was all nothing and that she was imagining things but she couldn't shake the feeling. The more she rode, the more she was sure someone was following her. She didn't even know why.

She shifted in her saddle a little and patted Bunny's mane.

"Such a good horse," she told her. "You have to put up with me and all my *qualish,* and you do it without even protesting."

As the sun hit the middle of the sky she stopped

for lunch. She looked for a place to set up and she heard a noise again. She froze in her saddle. Bunny continued along. A few seconds passed and she pulled on Bunny's reins to stop her.

Hisime took a deep breath and jumped off her horse.

She looked again for the source of the sound but she didn't see anything. All she saw were a few trees and a few boulders and rocks. There were some birds, too, but she didn't see anyone or any big game that could be the cause of the noises she heard.

Hisime thought about the stories she had heard of Wizards and Sorcerers, but she wasn't sure she believed in all that. Oh, sure, she had some small resemblance of magic from being part Elf, but to be able to control elements was just fairy tales. There had to be *something* out there—something *real*. Whatever it is, she thought, doesn't want to be seen.

She took a deep breath and got back on Bunny. She contemplated going back to Ardell where she wouldn't be alone anymore. She would, however, have to admit defeat in finding Jepith and she didn't want to do that. She couldn't do that. Calabmore would lose all faith in her, and that was all that kept her going.

She had always felt like a failure and now she would have to go back to the city and everyone else would know she was a failure—her friends, her brother, they would all be so disappointed in her.

She closed her eyes and took a deep breath. No, she wasn't going to fail this time. She opened her eyes and clenched her fists. "No, Bunny, I am not going to chicken out. I'll do this. I'll find Jepith and bring him back to Ardell for his crimes. I am going to do this."

With that she hopped back onto Bunny and start-

27

ed to ride off again, this time with new determination running through her.

PART THREE

ISIME WAS GETTING TIRED OF THIS. HOW IN *Forain* was she lost again? She wasn't this bad with directions. She knew she wasn't. There was no way she could be. She had always been good with directions, but this time she found herself lost in Emyn Toril. She'd been there about two days now and she was sure she had found Jepith's tracks.

But they seemed to be leading her around in circles.

Numerous times she had seen the same tree and after what seemed to be the third time, she had marked it with a simple rune and continued on. It should have been such a simple track to follow—

men's boots, Jepith would be on foot in his boots. She looked up and found her rune on the tree. Sighing, she walked over to the tree and put the fifth hash mark on it then leaned against it closing her eyes. Circles indeed.

She continued on again, following the boot marks. She was positive they were the same ones she had seen while leaving Ardell. The same boot tracks that had led her to the east sea. She scanned the ground for more prints but found nothing. Instead, she found broken twigs, rocks out of place, crunched up leaves, all of which were heading north. Well, it was the right direction, she told herself.

She hopped back up on Bunny and started to follow the tracks once more. She couldn't find the boot tracks again though, just signs of someone or something heading north. Following the tracks for about an hour, she came to another tree she had marked with a small rune. This tree only had two hash marks on it.

Jumping off Bunny, she walked over to the tree and put another hash mark on it then scanned the area, looking for anything new. A short prayer to the *Hanna Er*, pleading for directions, escaped her lips as she examined the area. She saw her own tracks heading off in two separate directions. Ignoring them, she searched for another set of tracks, something different. There had to be something she was missing.

Looking around, she saw a new trail of broken twigs and rocks out of place. It wasn't easy to spot, only a trained eye could see them. Cursing herself for not seeing it the first couple of times, she walked over to the broken twigs. Broken by a Human foot, she thought. Elves were light steppers and animal hoofs and paws had a different force to them than a

Man's. Smiling she stood up and led Bunny on.

A curse escaped her lips when she found herself back at one of the trees with the hash marks. She was positive the last trail she took would lead her to a new trail, but here she was.

"I am a failure, Bunny."

The horse snorted. Hisime wasn't sure if this was an agreement or not, but she took it as one. She patted the mare's mane fondly and took the last path she had found at this spot. Watching ever closer, she went very slowly—so slow that she decided to dismount her faithful horse. Looking at every single bit of detail, she moved inch by inch looking at every detail before moving on. She went on like this for hours, getting tired and worn down, but still she continued on.

A DAY OR SO LATER SHE HAD YET TO SEE THE trees with hash marks on them again and her confidence was building slightly. However, there had been no signs of boot prints again either. Perhaps Jepith had ditched his boots? No evidence of that was found, but it was something she kept in her mind regardless. The twigs she found still looked to have been broken by a Man's boot.

Just as she was becoming frustrated at herself once more, she stumbled upon a new track. She dismounted Bunny to take a closer look. She sat on her heels by the new track. *Boot tracks...* No animal could make these. But they also seemed to be planted there. Jepith knew they were after him and it wouldn't be hard to fake tracks. Especially since he had so much time to do it before she got there. She stood up and looked to her horse.

"Well, Bunny, do we stop here for the time being or do we continue looking for him?"

The horse blew air at her.

"Fine, fine. I know you want to get home too. Trust me, this is not my idea of fun. I promise," she assured her horse. She looked around and sighed. "Getting home would be nice."

She had contemplated quitting and going home so many times already. She had been gone long enough now that they would believe she had given it a valiant effort. Long enough that they would believe he had merely out performed her. She was still somewhat new to this whole thing. Sure she was older than most when it came to getting their first solo mission, and few came back without their target, but some were bested. And she was the first known female Ranger ever recorded in history. That had to stand for something, right?

The horse shook her head and blew out air again. Hisime looked to her.

"What?"

Bunny rubbed her head against Hisime's shoulder and Hisime petted her.

"You are the best friend ever, Bunny."

She smiled at the horse and pulled out the last apple they had and fed it to her.

"Looks like traps need to be set up for food tonight."

The horse ate her apple happily. Hisime smiled and patted her mane.

Then, the sound came again. It wasn't the same sound anymore; it was different now. It seemed to come from up in the hills and it was rarely the same as the first two times she had heard it. She still couldn't shake the feeling that she was being watched though. She hadn't seen anyone yet, but there were now more places than ever to hide. She felt so stupid that she hadn't found the source yet—especially since the noises seemed to come more often lately. She had lost a whole day looking for and trying to track the source of the sound a few days ago and she didn't have much time to spare for such things. She was almost positive a person was stalking her. She didn't think Jepith was stupid enough to stalk her though. So, who else was it?

"Who are you?" she yelled into the sky. There was no answer but she felt a little better from yelling. "Where are you hiding?"

She sighed and got in her saddle.

She planned to keep heading north and hope to find more tracks—different tracks than the ones she had been following around in circles for a day and a half now. She gently urged Bunny on. The horse let out a snort, but complied with the request and began to walk along the trail Hisime lead her down.

HISIME AND BUNNY MADE IT A FEW MORE MILES up the almost nonexistent path. She had happily nibbled on her dry meat and cheese—what was left of it—as they rode. Hisime kept an eye out for any signs and kept an ear open for any more sounds. She noticed nothing, but she decided to go on a bit farther just to make sure she wouldn't have to circle back yet again.

Right when she was about to turn around, she saw a broken twig. She reigned in Bunny and when they came to a stop jumped off the horse. Carefully, she looked around for anything else out of the ordinary and with her slightly heightened eyesight she saw an indentation in the ground where the track was. It was the mark of either an Elf or a Man who was trying to hide their prints. She beamed. She'd found Jepith's path. It took everything she had not to celebrate right there and then.

"We got him, girl," she whispered to Bunny.

Studying the ground around her, she looked for more signs. It wasn't an easy task but she was able to track the slight indentations in the ground. It wasn't always clear where they were going and sometimes they stopped all together and she had to find them again, but she always found them again. This guy was good, she thought. But she was going to be better.

She went on foot pulling Bunny behind her as they walked. She was the predator and Jepith was her prey. She took precise steps and calculated movements, keeping her eyes on the ground as best she could and her ears tracking sounds as her eyes tracked everything else. There was nothing else that mattered, just the hunt.

The adrenaline was rushing through her veins. She smirked as she followed the path. Each new track—or out of place leaf, crushed leaf, or snapped twig—just added to the excitement. No one could stop her now.

Suddenly, the sound came again. This time in the form of metal to rock. It broke her concentration—it broke her excitement. The adrenaline shifted. She bolted upright and looked around. This time the person, if it was a person, had made their mistake. They didn't have time to hide. They had messed up and tripped. She recognized the person right away and it was *not* Jepith.

She froze.

Getting up was a man she knew from her childhood. He was much older now, as she was much older now, but the Rangers blood of old flowed through him. He was blessed with an extra-long life, like the rest in his blood line. He, however, did not look like an old man. He looked about forty. His hair just beginning to go grey, giving it a salt and pepper look. His body as muscular as ever. The look on his face full of disgust.

"Narnim," she choked out.

"Hisime," he said as he stood. It almost sounded like a hiss. She shrunk back.

This couldn't be happening. How had he been able to find her? This poor excuse for a man was forbidden to come near her, by not only the Elves, but the Rangers as well. Why was he here? She knew he had been released from prison a few years back, but never had she imagined to see him again. He had abused her for fifteen years of her life. She had been his slave, his punching bag, and an outlet for his anger.

This couldn't be happening.

Hisime started to hyperventilate. She swallowed hard and took another step back. She tripped over something and fell to the ground. She laid there frozen, looking up at him in disbelief.

He smiled at her.

She was a scared little ten-year-old girl again. Her little brother was outside playing with his wooden sword while she cleaned her own blood off the floor from the beating she'd just received. It had been her own fault really. She didn't mean to forget the clothes on the line when the thunderstorm came rolling in. The thunder cracked and she ran inside with her brother and they hid under his covers. The clothes that were drying were drenched and would need to be washed again. It was completely unacceptable.

That beating was the worst one yet. She cried while she cleaned, as black eyes formed and her nose throbbed.

If only her daddy would come back. They had told her that he was dead, but he couldn't be dead. He was too big and strong and brave to be dead. Any day now he would come back with her mom and they would be a family again.

The blow was unexpected and to the back of her already throbbing head. As she turned to see what had hit her she saw her guardian Sayrah standing over her with her hands on her hips.

"Little girls do not daydream. Little girls do their chores and they do them quickly." Then Sayrah turned and was gone.

"Dear sweet Hisime Ara," Narnim's voice snapped her back to reality. His tone was sticky sweet. He had used this tone with her before, when she had done things he didn't agree with and he was getting ready to lecture her. It had always been chilling when he used that tone. "I have missed you so much."

He was lying. She knew he was.

Memories were flooding her brain; images she had blocked out long ago. Suddenly, she was fifteen years old again and mucking out the stables. She had to do this once a week and she was ok with it as it gave her time with the horses. No, she wasn't allowed to touch the horses, which was a shame, because she did enjoy them. They were beautiful creatures.

Calabmore was also in the stables eating some bread and cheese for his breakfast and sitting on one of the stable walls. They talked as she worked. His green eyes glowing and his dimple showing.

Then it happened faster than she thought possible, he fell backwards into one of the stable stalls and there was blood. She had never seen so much blood. She called and cried for Narnim or Sayrah but neither one showed up. Lifting up her skirts, she ran to the house.

Without asking her why she was there or why she was running, the beating started immediately and it took everything she had to tell them that Calabmore was bleeding in the stables. Narnim rushed to look while Sayrah continued the beating, lecturing her on calling them when something like that happened and not leaving the poor unfortunate soul to lie there bleeding.

Luckily for Calabmore, it was nothing more than a broken nose and a fat lip. Not so lucky for Hisime was another broken leg from the beating she received.

Her parents were not coming to save her.

"I wasn't expecting you to find me so soon." His words snapped her out of her memories again. "I guess if I hadn't tripped up, you wouldn't have. My old legs aren't what they used to be. Now are they?" He smiled a cold brutal smile. "But I guess it matters not. You are close to where I needed you to be."

As he spoke, beating after beating repeated in her head. Lecture after lecture. Insult after insult. Her heart was thumping a mile a minute. She couldn't slow it down. She couldn't talk. She just stared at him wide-eyed.

"I'm sure you are wondering what am I doing here, right?"

She nodded as she got up on one arm and tried to scoot back a bit. She made it a few inches but he took another step forward.

"You ruined my life, you little wench," he spurted out. Any sweetness in his icy tone was now gone. Pure hatred dripped from his mouth. "My wife's life, too."

When Hisime was taken to the Elves twenty years ago, she had informed the Lord of the Elves, her cousin, Orodorn, of all the things that her guardians had done to her. Narmin had taken off and wasn't found for years after that. The Rangers of Erenville, though few in numbers, had found him hanging out in South Cape Town as a fisherman. Narnim and his wife were brought before Lord Orodorn, Hisime, Calabmore, Melrim, and a few other select Noble Elves and was given a sentence of ten years in a Human's prison, along with his wife.

She nodded. What else was she supposed to do? What could she say?

He looked down at her, still smiling.

"We figured we would pay you back for everything you did."

"My—my—my... My brother," she managed to say

"Your brother is dead."

"No he's not!"

"He died in a raid." He frowned.

"He didn't," she squeaked out.

"Oh, but he did. It was two days ago." He sighed. "Such a warrior's death. He died young."

"No, no, no," she murmured.

"There was an Orc attack in Adrell," he began. "Calabmore and his real team weren't too far from there as you know."

She shook her head. She wasn't going to listen to this. She started to hum to herself. He wasn't dead. She had just seen him. He was happy and alive.

"It started to rain. I doubt the rain made it this far up, but it was a downpour there. As the call went out your brother's patrol of Rangers rode as fast as they could to help." The louder she hummed the louder he talked. He sat on his knees next to her. "The city was surrounded by more Orcs then have been seen before. There was no way in or out of the city. Five or six clans had gathered. That's just an estimate, no one really knows. The city was falling fast.

"It was a terrible sight to see. There were many already dead by the time Calabmore got there. He and his twenty men attacked from behind. They slashed through the Orcs for a good while before they were noticed."

"Shut UP!" she screamed as she covered her ears—she didn't want to hear this. She feebly slapped at him. He merely smiled at her. He was now sitting next to her.

"But you have every right to know," he told her stroking a piece of hair away from her face. She tried to slap his arm away but he was to strong. He had always been stronger than her.

"The Orcs were quite ruthless, but so was your brother. He fought valiantly. Just like I had taught him. Willem and Cadiny went down first. Both were stabbed through their chests. Then Jobany went. Things didn't get better, but they kept fighting."

Hisime was now shaking and crying. She knew all of these men. Every last one of them had taken her in and treated her, a woman, as an equal. Taught her to use a sword and a sling. They taught her how to track and how to cook and start fires and use healing herbs. They were brothers as well.

"Harmen went next. Decapitated. The ground was covered in rain and blood. Both red and black. Your brother fought on. Each friend who went down reinvigorated him. Each death made him stronger. He took down five Orcs, six Orcs, ten Orcs. They littered the outside of the city. Your brother plowed through them as if they were mere blades of grass."

Hisime didn't know what was going on anymore. She was back in the little cabin on the plains. She was being lectured by Narnim for stealing a piece of bread. She was being beaten by him and Sayrah. She was sleeping on the bed of hay in the corner. Her whole body was shaking. Words kept penetrating through her ears.

Narnim's voice was soft but firm. He sounded almost caring, which only made it worse. He brushed another strand of her hair away from her face. She flinched.

"Oh, he fought valiantly." He was no longer kneeling next to her. She didn't know what he was doing. Her eyes were closed. She tried to drown out the world. She felt nothing. "He took down close to thirty Orcs himself as he fought. He assisted in even more deaths. The Orcs realized he was the greatest threat to them. They circled him. Five arrows pierced him and he fell to his knees."

She opened her eyes and could see that he was enjoying telling her this. He was relishing in the fact that her heart was breaking more and more with every word that he spewed forth. She felt like she was dead.

"He kept swinging his sword and even then took down two more Orcs as he fought for his life. He knew the end was neigh. Yet, he still fought. The rain pounded down and your brother drew his last breath. He couldn't watch from all sides and was stabbed through his back. It was a long painful death. As the city cleared out the dead after the battle, Calabmore was still alive and struggling for breath. Blood was pooled under him and splattered all over his dying body. I held him as he drew his last breaths. My tears washed away some of his blood. My words, were the last ones he heard as his soul left his body for all eternity to join the *Hanna Er* in Kalom's Realm."

Hisime laid there motionless. The tears falling down her cheek. She couldn't feel a thing. Her brother was dead. Her rock and foundation was gone forever. The only one who ever cared for her. There was Melrim, but they rarely saw each other—perhaps he didn't even really love her. He was just toying with her. Nothing mattered. The fact that she was being carried gruffly didn't even register in her mind.

Her body jerked as she was thrown into a cart. She blinked and looked around. What was going on? She tried to move. She was tied up. She couldn't move. It snapped her out of her numbness, but it was too late. She looked right to Narnim.

"And you won't live much longer than him, little Hisime." He closed a gate on the small cage behind a horse. "Oh no. His death was long and painful. Yours will be even more so."

"You spoiled Narnim's name," came the shrill voice of Sayrah. She walked over and poked at Hisime with a sword through the bars of the cage. They weren't deep cuts but they were fine ones that stung like *Forain*.

"You spoiled my name. We found you and now we will ruin your life." She stabbed at Hisime again. This time it was a deep cut to her thigh. Hisime screamed out in pain. Sayrah laughed. Narnim smiled widely.

PART FOUR

THE NEXT FEW DAYS WERE A BLUR OF PAIN to Hisime. There were daily beatings and they were no less severe than what she remembered from her childhood—they may have even been worse.

Her wrists hurt from being tied up and the rope was beginning to dig into her skin, letting her blood flow freely on to the ground. A few times she heard her bones cracking over her screams of pain.

Of course, it wasn't just the beatings that caused discomfort. She was so very, very thirsty. When was the last time she had a drink? She couldn't remember, but she was sure it had been even longer since she last ate. The grumbling of her stomach reminded her of that often.

The worst pain, however, was the emotional pain of losing her brother and her friends in an Orc raid. Her brother, one of her saviors, was gone forever—just like her parents. Hisime wasn't sure whether to believe Narmin, but she did know that Orc raids were not uncommon and there had been so much detail to his story.

Hisime spent most of the days mourning her brother regardless. There was a lot of crying going on inside the small cage that was pulled by a large brown mare.

Sayrah rode that horse while her husband rode a dapple mare next to her. They ignored her for the most part—except to occasionally beat her for no reason—as they rode through the bare wilderness. And Hisime was perfectly fine with that. She did however wish they would untie her. Her arms ached from being tied behind her back and her wrists hurt as the ropes were digging into them. Her ankles burned from the ropes tied tightly around them and her head pounded from all the crying. Then, of course, there was the deep gash on her thigh that hadn't been cleaned or treated. She was sure if she survived this—though she wasn't sure she would— she would lose her leg. Elves didn't die from old age or sickness, but they did die from mortal wounds. She had never seen an Elf with a missing limb; she was pretty sure she would be the first.

The pain coursed through her leg with every beat of her heart. Thump, thump, pain, more pain and it got worse every day that passed.

At the end of their ride each day, Narnim or Sayrah would take turns beating her. It was like when she was still in their care—only worse. The beatings lasted till Narnim or Sayrah were exhausted and then the other would take over. Most of Hisime's ribs were broken now as a result, which made it hard to breathe.

A lot of the times Hisime was so numb and so thoroughly in shock that she felt nothing. She would drift into a sleep of hellish nightmares. Nightmares of her time as a child with her guardians. But at least then she had her brother. Now she had no one. And no one knew where she was. For all they knew, she was still searching for Jepith.

Would anyone miss her? Was there anyone left to miss her?

She thought of Orodorn and Melrim—likely the only two people left in the world who might care where she was. She had spent five years with Orodorn and Melrim in the Elven city of Orodorn, named after her cousin. She had learned so much there with them but she had been gone for nearly twenty years, only seeing them in passing most of the time. When she first met them, they seemed to care for her, and they had always been so great and wonderful to her, but did they care enough to come find her? Would she even be alive if they did?

The cart and horse came to a stop knocking her out of her thoughts. The pain came back as it did and she tried to take short breaths but even those hurt too horribly. She closed her eyes and counted her breaths. One, two, three, fo… She screamed as the cage was rattled. It was still daytime and she wasn't sure why they had stopped. The cage rattled again. Hisime opened her eyes to see Sayrah shaking it as hard as she could.

"Still alive, little Elf?" Sayrah laughed. "Elf, my ass… You are nothing but a scoundrel and a liar and a cheat and you are still worthless and probably a little whore to boot."

Hisime laid there and listened to the insults. What more could hurt her emotionally? She almost felt like laughing at Sayrah's absurdity, but that would cause more pain. More than she wanted to try and handle right now.

"You are as worthless as ever. The Elves are morons for thinking you are more. They think they are better than everyone else—just like your whore of a mother. Your father could have done better than her. Your brother used to run around after Elves too. Apparently Men are not good enough for your family." Spit flew and hit Hisime in the face. She went to wipe it away, forgetting momentarily that she was tied up.

Narnim walked over to the cage. He looked to Hisime then to Sayrah. "Why are we wasting time talking to it?"

"I needed to get out some aggression," she said sweetly to her husband. "After everything that she put us through, she deserves it."

"What did I do to you?" Hisime somehow managed to say.

"No one said you could speak!" Sayrah yelled as she reached through the bars and pulled at her hair. Hisime let out a cry. Sayrah kept pulling and tugging. Finally, the tension let out and her head hit the bottom of the cage with a thud. Her head ached from where Sayrah had pulled out some of her hair and she closed her eyes and took a deep breath.

The cage door opened and she was pulled to the ground. She landed with a thud, groaning in pain as she rolled onto her back. Just as she'd gotten onto her back, the kicks to the ribs started. She grunted and screamed and let them have their satisfaction. The more she screamed the happier they seemed.

She wondered if they would get bored with beating her if she just submitted to it. She wasn't sure, and had no real way of knowing so she just let the screams and the cries out.

She didn't know how long the abuse went on but it felt like an eternity and when the kicks and punches finally stopped, it felt like heaven. She could almost breathe again. Narnim scowled at her and kicked her one last time.

"Get up." He scowled at her.

"I can't," she coughed out.

"I said, get up!" He grabbed her by her hair and pulled her to her feet. He helped her back into the cage by throwing her in. Her shins hit the bottom of it and she fell in face first. Narnim pushed her legs in and then locked the cage again.

Within minutes they were rolling once more and each bounce and sputter on the road brought pure agony. She wanted to die. She wanted to be with her family. She wanted to know true happiness. Instead, however, nothing but pain came to her. She had to succumb to the pain; she had to find relief somehow. Every bone in her body had to be broken by now and she had patches of hair missing. The wound in her leg was now full of dirt and she knew it would start to fester soon enough. She was sure it would be her downfall.

She didn't know how long she passed out for, but when she came to, it was night fall and they had once again stopped. As Hisime looked around, Narmin and Sayrah were nowhere to be seen, but that wasn't saying much since one of her eyes was now swollen shut leaving her with limited eyesight. It hurt to move too much, so she closed her eyes again. It didn't get rid of the headache but it helped.

"It's just up the road a way. If we take her there

in the cage, people can track our wheels. It's why we stopped," she heard Narnim explaining.

"Are you going to carry her then?" Sayrah asked.

"No, that can be tracked too."

"So what do we do?"

"I am not sure."

"Can't you cover your tracks? You are a Ranger."

"I guess I can try." Hisime heard him sigh. She still couldn't see them and she wondered where they were taking her, and who would be tracking them. Were Melrim and the other Elves looking for her? Could she leave something for them to find her? Or where Narmin and Sayrah just being cautious?

"I'll carry her and try to keep to a less conspicuous path. Makes it hard to follow us. It will take a lot more work, especially since you broke her legs."

"Oh, she's fine. If she really is her mother's child, she is probably close to healed anyway."

"I told you it doesn't work that way. They don't heal faster."

"They are magical. They have to heal faster."

"Mortal wounds kill them. They don't regenerate, though."

"Why do you care?"

"I don't. I just… Oh, it doesn't matter."

The talking stopped and the next thing Hisime knew there were boots in her vision. She tried to look up but it was a blur. She was sure it was Narnim though. Sayrah didn't wear boots.

Hisime coughed a little, tasting the metallic aftertaste of her blood as she spit some out.

"Come on, you," he said, and then not so carefully, he hoisted her up onto his shoulder like a sack of potatoes. She whimpered and moaned. "Oh shut up."

THE NEXT BIT OF THE TRIP WAS A BLUR. IT WAS just her and Narnim. He carried her along the terrain in a very tedious manner as he tried to keep to areas where it would be hard to track them.

Other times, he stopped to covered their tracks. He would lay her down and go back over their tracks and clean them up—at least that's what she thought he was doing. He had no fear of her running away either. She could barely move, let alone run. She merely laid there alone, most of the time crying.

Every time he came back and hoisted her back over his shoulder the pain started over again. Narnim barely seemed to notice her, though. He didn't talk to her, didn't make eye contact with her, just walked along carrying his burden.

By night fall, Narnim's exhaustion started to kick in and he laid her down and looked at her. He didn't say a word. He just looked at her. He tilted his head and then pulled out his pipe and started to fill and light it. He watched her as he took a puff. There was no contempt in his look. There was no adoration either, but no contempt. Hisime tried not to tense up as she prepared herself for another beating. Every part of her body hurt, even her hair hurt.

"If I look hard enough, I can see him," Narnim stated nonchalantly.

"Who?" Hisime choked out.

"Your father. I can see the human in you," he said it almost like it was a compliment. *Almost*. "No filthy Elf in you."

"Calabmore was part Elf." It hurt to talk, but maybe she could finally get answers. She felt she could die and it would be all right. As long as she got some answers.

"Calabmore was your father's son as much as you are your mother's daughter." The contempt was back. "Calabmore was no more an Elf than you are a Man."

"I am half-Man. Calabmore was half-Elf."

"Maybe by blood. But attitude and demeanor ... you are as snooty and stuck up as any Elf. He is as noble and valiant as any Man. You have always thought yourself superior than everyone else." She wanted to laugh. If there was one thing she was, it sure as *Forain* was not superior to others. "Just like your mother," he continued.

"You hated her."

"She hated me."

"I can see why."

She didn't regret saying it. Not even a little bit. Sure the punch to her face was horrifying and the agony was barely tolerable, but it was worth it. She couldn't fight; she never could. She never expected to be able to face her fears. She was living her worst nightmare, and she was dying at her guardians' hands. She wasn't going down without some sort of fight though. It wasn't the greatest shot and she knew that it was a lost battle, but she did, however, give out a blow—even if it wasn't a physical one.

She spit out more blood.

"Always ungrateful. Always the mouth."

"I never did anything to you," she whispered. She wasn't even sure it came out until the next wave of pang coursed through her face.

"All I ever di—" She couldn't finish. She began to cough uncontrollably. Oh the torture of it all. She was ready to die. "All I ever did was live," she whispered through the pain.

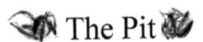

Then, the blackness took her.

PART FIVE

ISIME LANDED WITH A THUD AND ALL LIGHT left. She wasn't awake much longer, but when she finally came to, it was pure torture. Pain, agony, torture, misery, stitches, spasms, convulsions. Aches, cramps, soreness, and throbbing. Hunger and thirst.

She couldn't tell if she was alive or dead. If she was dead, she was surely in *Forain*. If she was alive, she was in a living *Forain*. She didn't know how long she had been in the darkness, but it seemed like an eternity. The cold, damp, darkness surrounded her. She could see nothing. She thought she could hear water dripping—from where, she didn't know. There was no light anywhere.

It hurt to breathe. Even more so than before. Before, it hurt because her ribs were cracked. Now, the very air burned her throat, her mouth, and her nose. The taste of the air was foul, rotten even. *Hanna Er*, it burned her eyes. The festering wound on her leg seemed to get worse from the air alone—if you could call it air. It burned her lungs. She coughed and wheezed and burst into tears. What had she done to deserve this *forain*?

She blinked her eyes a few times. The air hurt her eyes as well. Her life, her pain, her torture, apparently wasn't enough. She had to be put in this place. This darkness. This nothingness. Water continued to drip from somewhere. It was coming from more than one spot. Her ears were about the only thing on her that didn't hurt.

Her dry, burning throat yearned for the water. How long had it been since she had a drink? How long had she been gone now? A day? A week? A year? She didn't know. That was about how long she had gone without water though. Oh, the sweetness of water. The wetness of water. She could imagine it running down her throat. She closed her eyes. She could feel the wetness seeping down into her barren throat. It felt like heaven.

Wait!

Where had the water come from? She could still hear it dripping, but her throat was scratchy once again. It hurt from being so dry. Every swallow was agony. Where had the water she was drinking gone too? Was she drinking water? Of course she had been. But where did it come from and why was her throat so dry now if she had been?

Drip, drip, drip.

THE WATER TAUNTED HER. HER THROAT BURNED. Her stomached growled. Food. Nice succulent roast beef. With potatoes and carrots. There was no moisture left in her mouth to make it water. The heat of the meat felt warm on her throat. It soothed her throat and it tasted wonderfully. It was a nice tender beef. It was juicy and the juices helped water her arid mouth. Her stomach … was still empty. There was no meat.

What was going on with her? Was she hallucinating? She had to be. She coughed and whimpered. She closed her eyes. It didn't matter see saw the same amount. It was so dark. So dark. Her eyes hurt. The air hurt her eyes. She coughed again. The dripping continued.

She fell victim to unconsciousness again.

ETERNITY TICKED ON.

HER THROAT WAS SO DRY. SHE HAD TO GET TO the water. The dripping kept going. It woke her up again. Or at least she thought it woke her up. She drank from the pond that was by her as she laid there. It pained her to move her hands to cup the water, but she cupped it and drank. The cool water ran down her dry throat. It was the most refreshing thing she could ever remember drinking. Elvish fire whiskey had nothing on this water. Clear and crisp and full of flavor.

Her throat was on fire. There was no water. Nothing was there. She looked to the pond and it was gone. Nothing but dirt.

She blinked a few times. It didn't help. The pain was still in her eyes. She tried to move but that sent a coursing jolt of pain through every bit of her body. She screamed and cried out. She had to get to a point where she could move. She gritted her teeth and tried to move toward the dripping again. More pain. And she fell under the curse of unconsciousness once again.

THERE WAS NOT ONLY A REFRESHING POND TO indulge in, this time, but a whole feast as well. Calabmore was sitting not far away with Melrim and Orodorn. Willem and Cadiny and Jobany were there too. They were feasting on roast duck and baked potatoes and vegetables. There was wine and Elven fire whiskey by the cask. Cadiny laughed as Willem tried to drink the fire whiskey. He choked it down. Melrim and Orodorn just shook their heads at him. Elven Fire whiskey was hardly tolerable by Elves; Men Folk would instantly be drunk off just a few drops.

Calabmore looked to her and smiled.

"Hisime!" he yelled out cheerfully.

"Calabmore?" she asked confused.

"Of course it's me silly."

She stood up and walked over to him and…

PAIN. She fell to the ground. Calabmore and the rest disappeared along with the food and drink. The laughter died and faded away for good. What was going on?

She laid there in throbbing, agonizing pain and stared up at what she thought was the ceiling. She was breathing hard and trying to swallow. The pain over took her again.

DRIP, DRIP, DRIP.

SHE LAUGHED THIS TIME. SHE JUST WANTED A drink but she couldn't get to the water. She couldn't quench her thirst. Nothing was going to help her. The dripping made her laugh again. It couldn't be that far away.

DRIP, DRIP, DRIP.

HER EYES WERE STARTING TO ADJUST TO THE darkness and she could almost make out the hole she was in. It was still dark, but she felt like she could see the dirt walls and floor. See the wood covering the hole. Was that green fumes permeating the air? She couldn't tell. She wasn't sure.

DRIP, DRIP, DRIP.

MELRIM LAID NEXT TO HER HOLDING HER TIGHT. He was feeding her grapes and watermelon. They didn't say a word. She just ate. Then she ate some more. It tasted so good and was so wonderful and Melrim was so warm. The fire danced in his grey eyes. He stroked her hair and kissed her. Then he fed her another bunch of grapes.

"Anything else, my love?" he asked.

"No, this is wonderful," she replied.

"We have wine."

"No, the grapes and watermelon are heaven." He kissed her forehead.

"Care for a dance?" he asked. She giggled a little and he helped her up.

PAIN.

She fell down again. Her legs couldn't hold her. Melrim disappeared. She laughed. All that was around her was the dirt walls again. All she could hear was the dripping again. She had to get to the water.

DRIP, DRIP, DRIP.

SHE GROANED AWAKE. HER HEAD HURT SO BADLY. Her eyes hurt so badly. The dripping was driving her crazy. She just wanted a drink.

"SHUT UP!" she cried out and immediately

wished she hadn't. It didn't help anything. She still laid there in a heap of broken bones.

She carefully and slowly ripped a piece of her shirt off. The agony coursed through her arms and fingers but she had to keep at it. She gritted her teeth. *Remember your training*, she told herself over and over. She took the cloth and put it between her teeth and clamped down on it hard.

Pulling herself up on her arms, she moved a fraction of an inch toward the dripping. She was sure she could see it now. Her eyes had adjusted well to the dark. It didn't help the pain but she just bit down on the rag and moved another inch. Then another. Then she fell down and the pain took her over once more.

DRIP, DRIP, DRIP.

"SHUT UP!" she cried out as she awoke.

The rag had fallen out of her mouth as she had slept. She had to find it. She looked around and Calabmore knelt next to her and handed it to her.

"Just a little farther," he told her.

"You are dead," she muttered but bit the rag.

"You can make it," was his only reply.

She nodded and moved another inch. Then another. He kept encouraging her. With every reassurance he gave her, she made it that much closer. Inch by inch, boost by boost she made it closer to the dripping—closer to refreshing wetness for her dry mouth.

She reached out and drip. Right onto her finger. She brought it to her mouth. It was the most deplorable taste of water she had ever placed in her mouth … and it was pure heaven. She inched close enough to lay under it with her mouth open and drank every drop.

She smiled.

When she awoke, she found her eyes burning more than ever. They were wet from the water dripping onto them. She must have dozed off and moved enough for the water to drip onto her eyes in her sleep. She groaned a little and moved for the water to hit her mouth again.

"I told you, you could do it," Calabmore was sitting next to her smoking his pipe. "You did amazing." His dimple appeared and she smiled too.

"Are you an angel?" she asked him.

"I am whatever you need me to be," he told her. "I am your dream."

"No, you are real," she told him.

"As real as I can be."

She laid there drinking and watching him smoke till she dozed off again.

Eternity ran on.

Hisime was in a ball gown. A very nice candy-apple-red ball gown. Melrim was at her side in matching noble robes. His hair was tied back with a golden cord and both had elegantly braided hair. She didn't know how she got there but it was fine with her. She smiled and snuggled up to him and bathed in his scent.

"Oh, Hisime, I am so glad you found someone to love," came a strange woman's voice—but it was familiar, not really strange at all. But she didn't understand how. Opening her eyes, she saw a taller, fairer version of herself, except her eyes were green and her hair was silver

"Mother?" Hisime asked.

"Of course, darling." And she was pulled into a hug. Warmth spread through Hisime's body.

"But you died. You were killed…"

"I got … lost."

"Nonsense, Shalendra; you do not get lost. You were more than just lost," a man said with a laugh, he looked almost exactly like Calabmore, except his hair was salt and peppered and he was older.

"Oh, Daddy." Hisime said and hugged him close, never wanting to let him go.

"I have missed you, Hisime. Drip."

That was strange. Why had he said drip?

DRIP, DRIP, DRIP.

SHE RUSHED BACK TO THE PIT.

DRIP, DRIP, DRIP.

Hisime lost all track of time in between her fits of hallucinations and consciousness. The water was no longer tasty, but it kept her mouth wet. Her body still ached, but it was feeling better as her bones mended back together over time. Pain started to diminish, but remained relevant.

Her hallucinations came more often. Calabmore sat next to her, talking with her most of her days. They talked of nothing and everything. She almost felt good for the first time since she laid her eyes on Narnim. She would never live without pain ever again, but her body was learning to manage it.

As she laid there talking to Calabmore, a blinding light permeated her personal *Forain* and she closed her eyes. It was coming from above but she could see nothing. Even as she closed her eyes, the light was still blinding.

"I found her!" She heard a familiar voice call loudly. "I need help; she's down deep."

"Did she fall?" She heard another very, very familiar voice say.

"No, she was definitely put here. Now come on and help me get her out."

She opened an eye toward the blinding light and saw Calabmore. He was right next to her though. She looked over and he was gone. She looked back up and saw another face looking down at her. Melrim.

She smiled.

PART SIX

WHEN HISIME WOKE UP, SHE WAS LYING IN A nice bed in her room in Orodorn. It had been over a decade since she'd been in her room in the Elven city but it was just how she had left it; the servants had kept it clean while she was away.

She was beyond grateful to be back in a familiar setting. The window was open and shining brightly, and she thought of going over and looking out for a moment, until the remembrance of the pain she was in came flooding back.

How had she gotten to Orodorn was hardly more

than a fleeting memory in her head. She remembered hallucinating her brother and a blinding light and then pain—more pain. She thought that was odd, because when the light came she had already been in so much pain, but, somehow, she hurt even more. The entire time in that hole there had been so much pain that she didn't think it could get worse, but it did.

Everything that happened after that was a blur. She remembered bouncing around and someone trying to keep her from moving. She wanted it to be her brother. He had died, though. That much she remembered.

She vaguely recalled a second person who reminded her of Melrim, but he was off doing Lord Orodorn's work. He wouldn't have had time to save her from that hole. She had bounced in and out of consciousness so often she didn't know what was real and what wasn't anymore. For all she knew she was hallucinating right now and she was really still in that dark, damp, pit.

She remembered feeling massive amounts of pain as they re-broke limbs to re-set them—or at least she thought she remembered that. They did both of her legs and one of her arms. Her fingers on her left hand and two on her right were also re-set. With each new break she popped awake long enough to see who she thought were blonde Elves standing over her. The jolt of agony made her believe it was all real. She wanted it to be real. If it was real, then she was out of the hole. If it was real, she wouldn't have to suffer any longer—if it was real.

She tried to sit up but she was still in a fair amount of pain. She closed her eyes. She still saw light. She saw the red skin of the inside of her eyelids. She opened her eyes. There was no difference in the amount of light. She looked around. It had to be noon. It was so bright. She hadn't even noticed it before. She closed her eyes again—the same amount of light, and she could see everything on the inside of her eyelids. There was no darkness. What was going on? She opened her eyes again.

She didn't have time to think about it any longer as a knock came to her door and it slowly opened.

She couldn't believe her eyes—Melrim. She beamed to see him. He was definitely a sight for her sore eyes. His long black hair was hanging loose. He never let it loose unless he was relaxing for a few days. He wore his elegant red robes; her favorite of his robes. His grey eyes met hers and for a split second she could see them go wide. Then she saw life jump back into them. He beamed.

"Oh my, Hisime," he said jubilantly. He walked over with vigor in his step and sat next to her. He wanted to hug her. She could see the pain in his eyes come back and he clenched his fists and took a deep breath. "I will find him and he will face justice."

"Who?" The word was barely audible but his Elven ears picked it up.

"The person who did this to you." He ran his hand over her hair.

"Narnim."

"Shhhh." He began to place a finger over her lips but stopped himself, hesitant to touch any part of her. She was grateful for his consideration but she just wanted him to hold her. She started to cry. Melrim watched. The room remained blindingly bright.

THE NEXT TIME SHE WOKE, SHE AWOKE TO AN even more familiar face. She stared at it hard. A small dimple appeared on the face as she stared at him. It wasn't possible. He was dead. She must have been hallucinating again. No reason for it to stop now, just because she wasn't in *Forain* anymore didn't mean she wasn't going to keep hallucinating. Closing her eyes, she hoped the familiar face would fade when she reopened her eyes. The light still would not go away. She swallowed and then opened her eyes again, only for the face to remain there. The figure sat and watched with a smile as Hisime sized it up and down.

"It is me, Hisime," Calabmore said. Reaching out a hand she caressed his face. It felt real.

"Calabmore?"

"The one and only." He stood and bowed with a joking flourish. A small laugh escaped her lips as she tried to sit up, but winced instead. Eyes widening in fear, he ran over to help her. She clung to him, laying her head on his shoulder and closing her eyes—that cursed light! It wasn't just tears of pain and horror. No, her brother was alive and well and he was there holding her. The feeling of his fingers running through her hair was one of the best feelings in the world.

"He will pay for this, Hisime. I promise,"

"Shh." She didn't want to hear that name ever again and she wanted to think of him even less. Her life would forever be ruined by the scars that man left on her soul, and her body, and she didn't want this moment ruined by him.

She wasn't sure how long they sat like that, but eventually she fell asleep. She was so tired as her body tried to repair itself. So tired.

As she opened her eyes again, she found she was laying down on her bed once more. Calabmore reading a book sitting next to her. He smiled and put his book down to look at her.

"Morning, Sunshine." He smiled. "I don't know if I will ever get used to your new eyes." The last was to himself but she had heard every word he said.

"What about my eyes?" she asked softly.

He grumbled under his breath and stood up. "They shine."

"They what?"

"They shine."

He pulled a mirror out of her bedside table and handed it to her. With a shaking hand she took it and held it up to see her face and her eyes went wide. There was a glare from them on the mirror. They did indeed shine a piercing blue light—which explained the weird looks, wide-eyed expressions and the light that would not go away.

"No, no, no." she said softly.

"It's ok. I think they are cool. Do they … affect your eye sight?"

"So bright," was all she could get out.

Nodding, Calabmore stood up again and closed the curtains in her room. He was an amazing person, and she was so lucky to have him as her brother.

RECOVERY WAS A SLOW PROCESS. SHE SPENT MOST of her first week lying in bed being spoon feed. Melrim, and much to her surprise, Calabmore spent most of their time in her room with her. They were wonderful company.

She learned later that she had spent three weeks alone in the pit, and after that ordeal, any company was welcome. Lord Orodorn came by at least once a day to talk and Willem and Cadiny had stopped by too. Not one of them asked her about her suffering. Not one of them asked for details. They didn't pretend that it never happened; they just spared her the grief of reliving it.

The weirdest part of everything was the constant reactions to her new eyes.

"Your eyes are as gorgeous as ever, my love," Melrim stated when she asked him what he thought of them.

"Everyone keeps looking and me funny. They try to hide the looks but I see them."

"They glow, my love—like actual glowing. Of course you are going to get weird looks."

"They are far more interesting this way, and quite a bit more... What's the word, exotic? I love them," He said beaming as he kissed her.

Healers were constantly in her room and she asked them about her eyes, too, but the only thing they could come up with was that the toxic fumes in the swamp pit had messed with the *Kanolay* and transformed her eyes in more ways than mere super sight.

Calabmore, Willem, and Cadiny also finally told her the less interesting version of the Orc raid; the one where ten Orcs broke into Ardell in the middle of the night and stole five chickens and a cow. No one was ever in danger for their lives. They told her all about tracking down the Red Rot Clan members and disposing of them. She almost hated to admit that except for the ending she did like Narnim's version of events more. It was at least more interesting. The real story had almost put her to sleep.

Sleep was not so easy to come by, though. Her room was never dark anymore and it didn't help that she could see the inside of her eyelids now.

Melrim rarely left her side except to get her things. He even slept on the floor of her room in case she needed something in the middle of the night. The first few nights Calabmore had slept there as well. He soon moved to his own room next to hers though.

Calabmore left more often than Melrim did since he was helping Lord Orodorn with all the reports coming in on where Narnim and Sayrah were. The two were being tracked but Calabmore said neither had been found yet.

By the second week, Hisime was able to sit up in bed and talk better. She was getting used to the permi-light her eyes gave off and she was also able to breath without pain now. Her throat was no longer dry and scratchy and she could swallow without pain. Both her eyes could be opened wide now, and the once festering cut on her leg was healing. There would forever be a scar, but the elves had somehow saved her leg from amputation.

On the fifteenth straight day in bed, she had over-heard a conversation outside her room.

"They found them?" Melrim asked.

"No. Just her. She was at the bottom of a cliff. Her neck was broken," Calabmore explained.

"And him?"

"We don't know. His body wasn't found. We believe we found tracks heading toward the south west."

"To the Dwarves?"

"We don't know but the Dwarves hate the Elves and maybe he thinks he can find sanctuary there. Or maybe he's just trying to throw us off his path."

"You think he knows we are tracking him?"

"I think he knows that we will be searching for

Hisime. I don't know if he believes that we could have ever found her. He hid his tracks well around the pit. However, he seems to be lazy about them now."

"Well, at least one of them had justice served upon them."

Melrim then entered the room with Calabmore at his heels and nothing more was said. She didn't ask either.

By the end of the third week, she was up and learning to walk again. Her muscles had seized up and were tight. Her legs themselves had atrophied. Melrim gave them massages nightly and Calabmore walked her room with her every day. She was starting to hate her life again, but the Elven healers insisted she walk every day. She also started to feed herself again and even that was frustrating as her broken fingers and arm had also atrophied. How long had it been since she had used them now?

The best parts of her days were now part of the night. Melrim, who was still barely leaving her side and sleeping in her room, was given the ok from the healers to share her bed as long as he was careful. Most nights his arm would hover over her as he seemed to debate inwardly whether he should cuddle with her or not. He normally fell asleep without deciding, but she often pulled his arm over her and cuddled with him as he slept.

Sleep still didn't come easily for her but she didn't mind. She would stay up and watch him sleep; tracing the muscles in his stomach, his cheekbones, and the shape of his ears. She would kiss his forehead, his cheeks, his nose, and the tips of his ears, until she would finally drift off.

By the fourth week, Hisime was walking the halls, and by the fifth week, she was taking short trips out to the gardens with her brother and her lover—not necessarily with both of them at the same time. The fresh air did wonders for her and she was even walking mostly without support. Melrim and Calabmore still hovered incredibly close, but she was walking on her own.

By the sixth week, she was called into Lord Orodorn's quarters. She was always so nervous going into his office alone but she licked her lips and slowly made her way in. He turned and looked to her. He smiled and helped her take a seat.

"My dear Hisime Ara." He watched her as he walked to his own chair.

"Lord Orodorn," she said with a very slight bow of her head. She wasn't trying to be disrespectful, she was still very sore though. He didn't seem to mind.

"I don't want you to go into details, but it is time that you talked about what happened. I need to know who and why."

"Narnim and because I ruined his life, apparently." She wasn't making eye contact; she really didn't want to do this. She wrapped her arms around herself and Orodorn nodded.

"We figured as much from your early ramblings."

"Please, My Lord, I don't want to talk about this. Not now. Not ever."

"I understand," Orodorn said with a slight sigh. "However, you should know Sayrah Seregon is dead. We have reason to believe she fell down a cliff and broke her neck."

"I heard my brother and Melrim talking about it."

Orodorn frowned. "And Narnim?"

"You can't find him."

"We have found him. He was with the Dwarves,

as we predicted. He was hoping for sanctuary. When the Rangers of Erenville, Troop Ten-Fifty went asking questions,"—Ten-Fifty was the troop she belonged to; they were her friends and her family— "the Dwarves didn't deny that he was there. When they were told of the charges placed on him, they gladly handed him over."

"Why?"

"The Dwarves have no ill will toward the race of Men. They willingly help out when they can. I have a feeling that if my Elves had shown up, we would have been denied." He shrugged. "The point is, he is in our custody and headed to Erenville for trial."

"Why not here?"

"The Rangers got him, not Elves. He will face the justice of Men, not Elves. I have a feeling his punishments will be much harsher this time as well."

Hisime nodded. "Is that all, sir?"

"I guess so." He got up to help her.

"Sir?"

"Yes?"

"What happened to Jepith?"

The Elven Lord beamed at her. "He was caught and taken back to Ardell by Jobany."

She nodded and Orodorn helped her to his door where Melrim was waiting on the other side to assist her back to her rooms.

ABOUT THE AUTHOR

Misty Billman was born and raised in Aurora Colorado. She has a loving husband and son.